2004

# *SHELTER FROM THE STORM*

*To John-Peter and Janita,
who were too young to remember
the tornado that swept through Norwich
in 1998*

# SHELTER FROM THE STORM

CORNELIA KLOP

EARLY FOUNDATIONS PUBLISHERS

Published by:
Early Foundations Publishers
3130 Vanderbilt Road
Portage, MI 49024-6062 U.S.A.

ISBN 0-9742131-0-1

Illustrations by Mandy Stam

*All rights reserved.*
No part of this publication may be reproduced, stored in a retrieval system, or transmitted, in any form or by any means, electronic, mechanical, photocopying, recording or otherwise, without the prior written consent of the publisher.

# CHAPTER ONE

"Mom! Mom! Where are you?"

Alisha and Trevor come running into the house.

"Mom, where are you?" The whole family is sitting at the kitchen table, ready for lunch.

"We have helped Mrs. Hanson with her laundry, Mom. It blew off her clothesline. Is it ever windy!"

Alisha holds up her autograph book. "Look how nicely Aunt Jenny has written in my book! She has even drawn a picture of her puppy."

"Have you washed your hands, Alisha, and where's your bow?" Mother asks.

## Shelter from the Storm

Alisha's dark brown eyes first glance at her dirty hands, then at her braids. One bow is missing. She shrugs her shoulders. "I still had it this morning."

With one hand she tries to hide the dirt on her new yellow shirt. A dog jumped up on her this morning when she was patting it. The shirt is only a week old. She got it just before the summer vacation, on her last day of grade two.

Mom sighs. "Wash your hands and sit down. We have said grace already."

They quickly wash their hands and take their seats.

Two heads, one brown and one blond, bow. Although they are twins, they certainly don't look alike.

Trevor and Alisha pray aloud:

"Lord, bless this food, and grant that we
May thankful for Thy mercies be;
Teach us to know by whom we're fed:
Bless us with Christ, the living Bread, Amen."

Alisha takes a slice of bread and butters it. She hears the wind outside. "We helped Mrs.

## Chapter One

Hanson," she says again. "Her wash was all over the flower garden."

"I even had to climb a maple tree to get a green sock," Trevor says. He grins. "She was so worried I would fall."

"Tornado warnings are out," Heidi says. "I heard it in the drugstore."

"Tornado? What is that, tornado?"

Alisha looks at her sister. Heidi always knows so much. She is in grade four already.

"Tomato! Tomato!" cries Brian out of the high chair. Everyone laughs.

## Shelter from the Storm

There is so much wind with a tornado that houses and trees fall, right, Mom?" Heidi asks, looking at her mother.

Mom nods. "Yet it does not happen very often," she says when she sees Alisha's worried look. "I have never seen a tornado."

"Tomato! Tomato!" says Brian again. He points to his plate.

"A good idea, Brian," Mom says. "You'd better eat, Heidi and Trevor; you have to be at the dentist by three o'clock. Make sure you play around here. Grandpa and Grandma are coming to babysit."

"Yippee!" Alisha calls out before she licks some peanut butter off her knife. She quickly looks at Mom. Her mother does not see it since she is feeding Brian. Alisha loves it when her grandparents come.

"I am going to ask them if they want to write in my book, too," she says.

Mom reads the Bible. The chapter is about Samson and the lion. Alisha always likes that story. When Mom gives thanks, she asks if the Lord will spare them this afternoon, especially now when the tornado warnings are out.

# CHAPTER TWO

A little white car stops in front of the house. Alisha and Trevor run outside. Brian follows on his wobbly legs. Grandma gets out of the car, a blue purse hanging on her arm.

"Well, well, how big you've grown!" she calls out. "Come, give me a kiss. And you, Brian, what a big boy you are now!"

"Big boy, big boy," Brian says, raising his cheek for a kiss. After they all have had a turn, they go inside.

"Here it's much better than outside. Phew! What a hot, humid day!"

*Shelter from the Storm*

Grandma wipes her face with a handkerchief. Alisha looks at Grandma's leather purse. There is always something in it for them.

Grandpa has found a book already. He loves reading. He reads even while he is peeling potatoes for Grandma. He looks up. "How is my little girl?" he says.

"Little? I am seven already," Alisha exclaims proudly.

"Oh, that is right. How could I forget?" he

## Chapter Two

teases. Grandma opens her purse. Alisha wonders what will come out of it today.

"I have brought you some belly buttons, tiny little belly buttons."

"Belly button!" cries Brian, and he lifts up his shirt. He pokes his tiny finger into his stomach. Grandma pulls him close to her and hugs him. He watches her as she takes four little bags out of her purse. In all of them are wee little round candies, blue, green, red, orange . . . all different colors.

"Yummy! They look good!" Alisha exclaims. Grandma gives each of them a small bag.

"What do you say now?" Mom reminds them.

"Thank you, Grandma!"

"What about me?" Grandpa asks.

Alisha gives him a big hug and whispers in his ear: "Thank you, Grandpa!"

A little later Trevor and Alisha are playing outside in the backyard. They have a teddy bear and a horse in a cart.

"You know what?" Trevor says, his eyes twinkling. "I'll tie the wagon to the bike." He gets a strong rope out of the shed. Alisha helps him tie the cart and the bike together. It's not so easy, but it works. When Trevor gets on the bike and starts to ride, the bear and horse hop up and down in the wagon. Alisha laughs and runs along. Her braids are bouncing on her back.

"Now it's my turn," she says.

Just then Mother comes out of the house.

"Trevor! Time to go to the dentist," she calls.

Trevor stops suddenly, and the bear and horse go sailing through the air.

"Watch out, be careful!" Mom warns.

Alisha stays outside, but it's not so much fun now that Trevor is gone. "Oh, wait, I can look in my autograph book," she thinks. Alisha gets it and brings it outside. She sits down under the striped umbrella on the patio and looks at her book. She loves the blue color and the picture of the bear. Too bad Brian ripped out that one page. Dad has taped it back in, but it doesn't look as nice as before. Alisha opens the clasps and pages through it. Her Mom and Dad still have to write in it. She wrote their names on top of the first pages so no one else would take their places. She likes Joleen's page best of all. Of course, Joleen is her best friend. Alisha knows her poem almost by heart:

## Chapter Two

Peace be to you, my dearest friend
Many years of health and joy!
Love your Bible more than play,
Grow in wisdom every day
Like the dove that found no rest
Till it flew to Noah's breast
Rest not in this world of sin,
Till the Savior take you in.

Joleen even glued seven pictures on the page, pictures of farm animals. Alisha looks up to the sky. The sun is hiding. It is still hot, though.

She turns a page in her book. Esther did a messy job. She drew marker lines to write on. Then comes Aunt Lisa's page. She was the first to write in it, even before she gave the book to Alisha. She calls it a "poezy album."* "She is so kind," Alisha thinks. "I hope they will come from Holland soon again to visit us." She tries to read Aunt Lisa's verse, but reading Dutch is very hard. Alisha flips through the book. She notices how sticky her hands feel. Again she looks up. The air

---

*"Poezy album" is a blank autograph book.

## Shelter from the Storm

is so still. The book is almost half full already. Martha wanted to write in it too, but she had made some mistakes and glued two pages together. Sandy's page is next. It looks nice, but it took her so long before she gave the book back. Sylvia and Alisha are the only two girls in the class who have autograph books.

Grandpa comes outside to feed Bruno, the dog. He has rolled up his sleeves.

"You may write in my book too, Grandpa." Alisha looks up to him.

"Well, I hope I have brought my glasses. Otherwise, it won't work," he answers.

"You have them on your nose," Alisha laughs.

Grandpa laughs with her. "Tonight," he promises, "tonight I will write in it."

Alisha fastens the clasps and puts her book on the picnic table. She skips along with Grandpa to the doghouse. She sees Grandpa's worried look when he glances at the dark sky.

"You think we'll have a . . . a . . ." What was that word again? . . . that kind of storm?" she asks with a shiver.

"I don't know, but I don't trust it." In the distance they hear rumbling.

*Chapter Two*

"Thunder," whispers Alisha. She doesn't like thunder. Holding on to Grandpa's hand, she walks with him into the house.

## CHAPTER THREE

"We'd better start supper early, today. Can you help me, Alisha?" Grandma asks. "I need someone to whip cream."

"Oh, yes." Alisha beams. "I sometimes do that for Mom, too." She gets the mixer from the cupboard and plugs it in.

"Here, wear this." Grandma hands Alisha a flowered apron. Alisha starts mixing. Her red tongue sticks out of her mouth.

"You think it's ready, Grandma?" she wonders after a while. She raises the mixer, but forgets to turn it off. Oops! Big blobs of whipped cream fly all over the counter. Alisha looks at Grandma. Then she licks at some spots.

*Chapter Three*

"Alisha!" Grandma scolds and turns the mixer off. "Let me have a look at the whipped cream. Needs a bit more," she says.

Again Alisha hears thundering, louder than before. She turns on the mixer, but suddenly . . . the light flickers . . . everything is dark. The power is off. Alisha looks through the window. She sees the dark sky. It looks almost green. The wind is getting stronger, bending trees with its force. One of the flowerpots on the porch falls over with a crash. Grandma quickly runs outside. The door slams closed behind her. She grabs the two planters and carries them inside.

"Look at the squirrels, Grandpa, they've all come to the deck!"

When Brian hears that, he wants to see the squirrels too. He looks out and points to them. "Doggies! Doggies!" he cries out.

"I think we'd better go to the basement," Grandma says, and she picks little Brian up. Alisha follows her. Grandpa opens some windows and goes downstairs too. In the basement, it is quite dark. "Scary," thinks Alisha. They all sit on the carpet while Brian snuggles on Grandma's lap.

Alisha looks at Grandpa. She can barely see

his wrinkled face in the dark. His eyes are closed, and his lips move. He is praying, she knows. Grandpa loves the Lord. He is a child of God. Once, when he was really ill, the Lord gave him a new heart. Grandpa had told her about it.

Grandpa opens his eyes and smiles at Alisha.

"Are you afraid?" he asks.

She whispers: "Yes."

"The Lord can spare us." Grandpa says. "He sees us, everywhere, even here in the dark basement." Alisha folds her hands while she looks through the little window. She can see sand and leaves flying by.

"Lord, help us," she prays. "Help Daddy, and Mommy, and. . . ." Would Mom still be at the dentist's with Trevor and Heidi? Or on the way home maybe? she wonders. She hopes they'll come home soon.

The wind is howling. It roars like a huge airplane, flying overhead. The windows whistle and rattle. Alisha hears banging sounds outside, thumping and crashing noises. It sounds as though pieces of something are falling. What is happening? Everything is quiet in less than thirty seconds.

## Chapter Three

"I think it's over," Grandpa says quietly. "Let's go upstairs."

When they go outside, Alisha can't believe her eyes. The ground is covered with leaves. Big boughs have been ripped off the trees; electric wires hang down from the poles. Blown over the fence, Bruno's doghouse has landed in the neighbor's backyard. The white patio chairs are strewn all over. The picnic table is upside down. Their flagpole is tilted over, the Canadian flag still fluttering in the wind.

When Alisha looks towards the street, her eyes become as big as saucers. In the house across the road, the front windows have blown out; the curtains are blowing limply outside. Large spruce trees on the roadside are snapped in half. The neat grey-sided house down the road is missing a large part of its roof. It was ripped open by a maple tree that fell on the house. Another giant spruce is lying on top of Grandpa's car. Yet the sun is shining brightly. How strange!

Lots of people are walking in the street, talking excitedly, and hugging each other. Others are crying. Some men are taking pictures. The people have to step carefully over pieces of wood, scattered glass, and power lines. Alisha stays close to Grandpa.

Mr. Ward, the neighbor, walks up to them. "What a scare!" he says. "I was working in the garden. Just before the wind started, there was an eerie calm. You couldn't hear anything; not even a leaf was stirring. Then the strong wind started coming, and I saw a black funnel cloud heading this way. Crows were flying around. I did not stick around long enough to watch. I just dropped everything. I didn't think I could run that fast anymore, but I did make it to the basement."

Grandpa nods his head and says, "What a wonder! It could have been so much worse. The

## Chapter Three

Lord has spared us. He does not deal with us according to our sins."

Roger, a boy from Alisha's class, rides his bike over to them. He has a hard time getting around the rubble. "Did you see the tornado?" he asks Alisha, but he does not wait for her answer. He continues: "I heard something that sounded like a train coming. I looked out of the window and saw a big black thing coming toward me. I was afraid it was going to pick me up. It went right over our house. My mom thought she saw birds in the sky, but they turned out to be branches." He shakes his head, steps on his bike again, and leaves.

Bruno limps toward them. He licks Grandpa's hand and yelps. What has happened to him? A tall man in coveralls comes running. "The school is damaged," he pants. "A part of the roof has blown off."

Grandfather brings Alisha inside. "I am going to see if anyone needs help. Stay with Grandma."

## CHAPTER FOUR

Grandma is still sitting with Brian on her lap. She has her handkerchief in her hand. A worried look is on her face. They hear all kinds of sounds coming from outside: chain saws humming, people calling, trucks roaring, sirens shrieking . . .

Brian puts up his finger and says, "Listen. Police!"

The telephone rings. Grandma picks up the phone and hears Father's voice, "Are you all okay?"

"We're fine." Grandma says. "We hope the others will be back from the dentist soon. What time are you coming home?"

## Chapter Four

"I'm leaving right now," answers Father. "Hope to be there soon."

As Grandma hangs up, Mom, Heidi, and Trevor arrive. "We had to take another road because a big tree had fallen down!" Trevor says. "You know what? I was in the dentist's chair when the power went off. The chair couldn't move anymore. The dentist couldn't fill my teeth either. Now I have to go back another time." He shrugs his shoulders. "Oh, well. . . .

You should have seen the school, man. The third grade classroom has caved in. Lots of windows are broken. The bike rack was lying on the baseball diamond. Unbelievable! Lots of people were cleaning up already."

"Most stores were closed," Mom says. "We stopped at the corner store, which was still open. Was it ever busy! Everyone asked for batteries, films, or candles. The batteries were sold out in no time."

When Grandpa comes home, he says: "So far no one is hurt badly. One boy was taken to the hospital. A branch fell on his head, but he seems fine. It is a great wonder. Some houses are damaged quite badly. The community center is open for all people who need food and shelter."

## Shelter from the Storm

"Were there many people? Was there anyone we know?" Grandma asks.

"Mrs. Finnans from King Street was there, crying softly. She lives in that house with all the blooming plants on the windowsill. She had been sleeping on the couch when the telephone rang. She had not noticed the strong wind before. When she went to answer the phone, the tornado hit. Her living room ceiling is gone, peeled off

## Chapter Four

like an orange skin. There was debris all over; even her couch was covered. She was still shaking, but thankful that she was spared."

"Debris? What is debris, Grandpa?" Trevor, who is listening closely to everything Grandpa says, looks at him.

"That is all that is left over when something is destroyed. What you see on the street and in the backyard, that is debris."

Alisha sighs. She is happy she was at home when it happened. What if she had been outside, or at school, or . . . ? She shivers.

Father is late. When he comes home, he tells how hard a time he had getting into town. "The police stop everyone. If you do not live in Grandbrook, you cannot get into town. They want people to work, not to look. I couldn't drive the normal route either. Large trees were uprooted, blocking many streets. In the street behind us, with all the spruces, there is not one tree left. The baker's car has been tossed into their swimming pool."

"In the swimming pool!" Trevor whistles. "That must have been quite a splash."

They all sit down for supper.

## Shelter from the Storm

"I wonder when the lights will go on again," Heidi says.

"It might take a while, because the whole town is out of power," Dad answers. "At least our telephone is working. Many people do not have that either. At work we didn't notice much of the tornado, except that the power was off."

Father thanks the Lord for His sparing hand. It could have been so different. . . .

Supper is not like other times. Nothing warm today—cold chicken on bread, jello with whipped cream for dessert!

"If we don't have lights, you cannot write in my book tonight, Grandpa," Alisha says. "That's too bad."

Suddenly her eyes grow big. "My book!" she gasps. "My book . . ." Everyone looks at her. "My autograph book is still outside."

"Where is it?" Mother asks.

"I left it on the picnic table, but the table was upside down," Alisha says, as tears fill her eyes.

"I will take a look after supper." Father calms her down. "Maybe it just fell."

When Grandpa closes supper by reading from the Bible and praying, Alisha does not hear

## Chapter Four

much. She is still thinking about her autograph book. What if the storm blew it away?

Father goes outside right away. Alisha watches him through the window. She sees him put the table and the chairs upright again. While he picks up some twigs and stones, he looks around. Now and then he stoops down and looks under big branches. He puts large pieces of scrap metal on a pile. The neighbors are outside, too. Alisha sees her dad walk up to them. He talks to them. Maybe they've found it, she hopes. She looks closely, but the neighbors look around, shrug their shoulders, and shake their heads. Dad walks through the backyard once more before he comes back inside. "I can't find it now, Alisha," he says, "but tomorrow we will look again."

Alisha does her best not to cry.

Before Alisha and Trevor go to bed, Mother gives them apple juice. "We will drink it too since we cannot make coffee," Mom says.

It is getting dark. Grandma is busy with candles and matches. Four candles are lit already.

Brian is watching closely, his head tilted. "Don't touch, don't touch!" he says while his finger is slowly reaching for the candles.

## Shelter from the Storm

"You'd better not touch!" Grandma says.

Brian sighs and pulls his hand back. Grandpa gets a candle beside his reclining chair.

"Otherwise he can't read," Grandma says with a smile.

"I don't think I will do much reading tonight anyway," Grandfather says. "There is too much to think about."

At eight-thirty, it is time for the children to say "good night". Alisha can't sleep. She tosses and turns in her bed. It is so hot. She throws her sheet

## Chapter Four

off. Many sounds are coming from outside. Heavy trucks are driving past. People are talking. The wind roars. Is it getting stronger? Is the tornado coming back? What if her window is blown out during the night?

She grabs her sheet again and pulls it over her head. No, that's too hot. She thinks of her autograph book. Where can it be? Maybe it blew over the fence. Or maybe . . . You know what? She climbs out of her bed and tiptoes through the hall.

"Psst. Trevor, are you sleeping?"

"No, I can't sleep."

"Neither can I. You know what, Trevor?" she whispers.

"What?"

"Shall we look for my autograph book ourselves, tomorrow?"

Trevor thinks for a moment.

"Sure. Let's go right after breakfast. Don't worry. We'll look till we find it."

Alisha quietly walks back and crawls into bed again. Just in time! Downstairs a door opens and Mom's voice calls up: "Do I still hear someone? It's time to sleep!"

*Shelter from the Storm*

"Yes, Mom."

Alisha turns onto her stomach. Tomorrow, she thinks. Tomorrow I'll find my book.

# CHAPTER FIVE

It's early in the morning. The sun is shining brightly. Birds are singing in the trees. A brown squirrel is chasing a gray one. They both jump over to the walnut tree. Some nuts fall down on the roof of the shed, but Alisha doesn't hear it. She is still sleeping.

Listen! Soft, little footsteps pitter-patter through the hall.

"Lisha, Lisha!"

Alisha opens her eyes slowly. Who's calling her? Her teacher? Alisha had just been dreaming that her teacher had found her autograph book. It had been lying on the grass behind the school.

### Shelter from the Storm

"Lisha, move over!"

Oh, now she hears who it is. It's Brian! He always comes to her when he wakes up early. Sometimes he even comes in the middle of the night. Alisha moves over. Brian crawls into her bed. She puts her arm around him. "Shh, Brian, the others are still sleeping," she whispers. A little later she dozes off again.

"Lisha, froggie, froggie!"

Alisha frowns. What's Brian talking about? She sees him pointing to the toy box.

"Come on, Brian. Frogs are outside, not in the house." Brian gets a little mixed up yet with the

## Chapter Five

names of animals. Everything on the farm he calls a "horsee," and anything with wings is a "birdie". But then . . . Alisha sees something moving as well. What can that be? Hop, hop.

Brian slides off the bed. "Froggie, froggie," he calls out loud. He jumps up and down. Alisha takes a closer look. Brian is right! A real frog is hopping in her room. It's a little one, but it has very big eyes. They almost pop out of its head, Alisha thinks. Hop, hop. Look! It hops through the door opening.

Brian follows it quickly into the hall. He looks around. Where is the frog? "Froggie, all gone!" he says sadly.

Alisha peeks around the corner of the door. All of a sudden she sees the frog jumping toward her. "Help! Mom, a frog!" she screams. The frog hops to the staircase. There it stops, just for a moment. Now it jumps down. One step, two . . . then it stands still again. "Over there, Brian. There it is." Brian falls on his tummy and looks down.

The bedroom door opens. It's Dad in his bathrobe. He looks sleepy. "What's all this noise about? Can't you be a bit quieter?"

## Shelter from the Storm

"Yes, Dad," Alisha says, "but there's a frog in the house."

"Froggie, froggie," Brian calls out as he lies on his belly. He leans over the staircase.

"Be careful, Brian. Don't fall. Where is it?" The animal jumps down another step. "You are right," Dad says.

"I wonder how we got a frog in the house," Mom says, puzzled. She pushes her hair behind her ears and shakes her head. "Anyway, how do we get rid of it?"

"Let me do the job. I'll catch this toad for you." Dad goes down the stairs. He makes sure he doesn't step on the toad. A little later he is back with a canning jar in his hands. He lays it on the carpet, in front of the toad. The animal doesn't move. "Come on, little fellow, jump in. Don't be afraid. We won't hurt you."

In the meantime everyone is watching. Grandma comes along with a paper towel. "Here, this may do the trick." Sure enough, one little shove and the frog is inside the glass jar.

Dad closes the jar with a lid. "Now we had better give you some air." He pokes some holes in the lid with sharp scissors. He places the jar on

*Chapter Five*

the kitchen table. A little later, all four children are quietly watching the toad. It's trying to climb up against the jar sides. It doesn't work. It slides back again and again.

"I feel sorry for the frog," Grandma says. "It has hardly any room to move."

"Why do you call it a toad, Dad?" Heidi asks. "Isn't it a frog?"

"A frog has longer legs," Dad explains. "It can jump high, but a toad can only hop. Look at this toad. Its skin is dry and bumpy. The skin of a frog is smooth. Most toads live on land, while frogs can live in the water and on land. Come, let's bring the toad outside." The kids follow Dad. He lays the glass jar on the grass and opens it. The toad doesn't move. Dad shakes the jar a little, and the toad falls out. "It may be a bit afraid of us; move back a bit." Sure enough: Hop, hop, there it goes, into the flower garden.

"Now I know how it came into the house," Grandpa says. He smiles at Grandma. "You brought it in."

"Me?" Grandma looks at him in surprise. "No way. I wouldn't even dare to touch one!"

"Remember the flowerpots you took into the

*Shelter from the Storm*

house just before the storm? The toad must have been in one of them." They all laugh.

"It's a good thing it didn't jump out right away, Grandma," Trevor says. "You would have jumped too, I think!"

## CHAPTER SIX

After breakfast, Alisha, Trevor, and Heidi are busily working outside. Alisha and Trevor want to leave right away, but Mom has different plans. "Alisha, Trevor, and Heidi, why don't you clean up the back yard? The grass is covered. Pick up branches and twigs, leaves, and the other little pieces."

Alisha frowns at Trevor but does not say a thing. She knows complaining would be useless. Well, looking for the album has to be done later. In a short time they are all working outside.

Actually, now that they are working, Alisha has forgotten that she was a bit grumpy. She

## Shelter from the Storm

even forgets about her autograph book for the moment. The sun is shining brightly, although it is a lot cooler than yesterday.

Brian helps too. He holds a rake in his hands. Looking at the others, he tries to do the same as his brother and sisters.

"Look, Brian. This is how you should do it."

Trevor grabs the rake to show Brian, but Brian holds on to it tightly. He looks at Trevor with an

## Chapter Six

expression on his face as if to say: "Leave me alone! I can do it myself."

Alisha brings a new load of twigs to the road. The mayor has said that people should move fallen limbs and brush to the roadside. Big dump trucks will come to collect them. Bins are placed at certain spots where people can get rid of scrap metal.

After Alisha has dropped the twigs, she looks down the street. Many people are cleaning up their yards. Public work crews are clearing the streets. She sees trucks full of steel and lumber driving along slowly. Chain saws are still droning everywhere. Across the road, a number of people are taking a break. As they sit on their lawn chairs, they are drinking coffee out of foam cups.

I am thirsty too, Alisha thinks. I am going inside to get a drink. She walks toward the house. At that same moment, Grandma comes out the kitchen door. She carries a tray with drinks and muffins.

"Here, you all deserve a break. I can really see you have worked hard."

"Mmmm! Blueberry muffins."

Mom and Grandpa come outside too.

*Shelter from the Storm*

"I am surprised to see how much you have done! It is quite tidy already," Mom says. "I knew you could do it. Even Brian has helped, I think."

Brian points to the grass. He raises his hands: "All gone!"

"I am glad the power is on again," Grandma says, stirring in her cup. "I surely like my coffee."

"The power wasn't off very long. I think it came back about six this morning," Grandpa says. "Those people must have worked hard all night."

Alisha feels as though she's sitting on pins and needles. Why do grown-ups always have to talk so long? She and Trevor want to go to search for the book. She doesn't want to ask permission. Alisha knows exactly what her mom would say: "No, it is too dangerous. You will just be in the way of the people who are working." Not asking is safer, she thinks.

Finally everyone stands up and goes inside. Mom takes Brian along. Heidi follows them to help Grandma do the dishes. In no time Trevor and Alisha are on their way. Where will they start?

# CHAPTER SEVEN

The twins first walk to the neighbors and look over the fence. This yard has been all cleaned up already. Only the top of a pine tree is still hanging on the roof.

"It doesn't look as though the book is here. Let's go on," Trevor says. They walk together to the next house. Some men are walking on the roof. They are pulling a big piece of tarp over the house. The back porch and top floor windows have been blown out, and some workers are nailing wooden boards in front of the openings. Trevor and Alisha watch the workers for a while. When an older lady comes out of the house, Alisha walks up to her.

## Shelter from the Storm

"Have you seen my book?" she asks in a small voice. The woman keeps on walking. Alisha doesn't know what to do. She first looks at Trevor, then she follows the woman and tries again, a bit louder this time: "Have you seen my autograph book?"

The lady looks at Alisha in surprise and says in a kind voice: "Your book, my dear? Did you lose your book? No, I haven't seen anything like that. What is your name? If I find it, I will let you know."

The twins move on. There is the park where they always play. Look at the swing. It's toppled over. A walnut tree is lying on top of it. The benches in the park are still in the same spot, but they are covered with leaves and twigs. You can't even see the path that runs through the park anymore. County workers are feeding branches into a truck. The branches are being chewed into little pieces.

"That is handy!" Trevor exclaims when he watches it. "A lot more will fit into the truck now." Alisha gets off the sidewalk onto the field.

"Out of the way, kids. This is no place for you right now. In a moment the wood chipper will be

## Chapter Seven

leaving. It is too dangerous out here. Get!" One of the workers points to the road with his thumb. The twins leave.

When they turn round the corner, they notice a little red car with speakers on the top. A man is standing beside it with a large camera in his hand. He is talking to three or four people. What can that be?

"I think it is a man from the radio station," Trevor says. "Let's go and listen." Alisha and

## Shelter from the Storm

Trevor walk a bit closer. The man with the camera is asking the people questions. One man is saying: ". . . When I saw the funnel coming toward me, I jumped out of the van into the ditch. I saw two pieces of sheet metal and a bike up in the air. I was shaking more than my car was shaking. I didn't know what to do. I prayed to God . . ."

Alisha and Trevor look at each other. This man must go to church too.

Now a woman tells her story: "We were having coffee in our kitchen. My husband was saying how he enjoyed the rain after the dry spring. Suddenly my son ran in and yelled: 'The shed is down.' We went to look. It was true, but we were lucky. The cats were okay, and even the raccoon survived . . ."

The two children are now standing right behind the little group. Suddenly the man with the camera places a little speaker in front of Trevor: "Hello, my young fellow. Where were you yesterday when the tornado hit?"

For a moment Trevor is too surprised to answer. Then he replies: "I was in the dentist's chair."

## Chapter Seven

"Did you notice anything?"

"I guess so! All of a sudden it was dark. A man came running through the hall and screamed, 'Tornado!' The dentist lifted me out of the chair because it would not move anymore, and we ran to the basement. I tripped in the dark, but someone grabbed me. We heard many funny sounds. I didn't know what it was. When we came upstairs again, they took my bib off. Now I have to return some time to get my fillings. My mouth was pretty sore from the needle."

"Thank you, you are a brave boy," the man with the speaker says, and he pats Trevor on the shoulder.

"What do you remember of the tornado?" he asks Alisha. She thinks a moment. "The wind . . . , the sounds, all the trees that fell down, and the wind blowing away my book."

"Your book?" the man asks.

"My blue autograph book. It was on the picnic table, but after the storm it was gone. We are looking for it now."

"Well, if I hear about a blue book, I will tell you. Where do you live?" After Trevor and Alisha tell him the name of their street, they go on again.

## Shelter from the Storm

A huge crane comes by, followed by a truck loaded with huge beams. The children wait for it to pass by, and then they cross the street. Wherever they look, wherever they ask, no one has seen the book.

"We might as well go home. I don't think we'll find it," Trevor says.

"Let's ask in one more place. There is someone in the yard over there; maybe she has found it," Alisha says hopefully.

"I doubt it," Trevor mumbles. The woman is busy cleaning up the garden.

When Alisha asks the question, she hardly looks at the children. In an angry voice she says: "Hurry up, go! I've better things to do than look for a book!" Alisha turns around as quickly as she can. She is scared of this unfriendly lady.

"I told you," Trevor says and heads for home. Alisha follows him.

I don't think I will ever see my book again, she thinks sadly. If only I had not left it on the picnic table.

# CHAPTER EIGHT

Just before Trevor and Alisha turn into their street, Trevor looks at his sister.
"Here is King Street. You know what? Let's go to Mrs. Finnans' house. We'll just walk over, have a quick look, and go home."
When he crosses the street, Alisha follows. "Her living room ceiling was peeled off like an orange skin, Grandpa said. I wonder what that looks like."
A little later, the twins are standing in front of the house. They pay no attention to the green pickup truck in the driveway. They just stare at the house. It does look awful. No wonder Mrs.

## Shelter from the Storm

Finnans couldn't stay there any longer. There is hardly a window left which is not broken. The chimney has fallen down. What a mess! "See, Trevor. There is that couch Grandpa was talking about." Alisha points with her finger to the back of the living room. "And look, all her flowerpots are in pieces on the floor."

"We had better go home now." At the exact moment when Trevor pulls Alisha away from the house, they both hear the same sound, coming from inside: "Ah-choo! Ah-choo!" It sounds loud through the broken windows.

Alisha stops in her tracks.

Trevor looks at her. "Did you hear that?" he whispers. Without another word they both start running away from the house.

"What's the hurry?" A dark voice booms when they run around the corner. Oops, they have almost bumped into their neighbor.

"In Mrs. Finnans's house . . . we heard someone sneezing. A man was inside. It must be a . . ."

"Well, maybe somebody's visiting her."

"No, she isn't home. She can't sleep in her house because of the tornado."

## Chapter Eight

Mr. Ward starts walking in the direction of the house.

"Come along, I'll have a look. You can show me where it is. If it looks suspicious, I have my cell phone with me, and we'll call the police. Which house is it? That white one with the blue shutters? With the pickup in the driveway?"

The twins nod. Just at that time a man walks out of the gate with a big lamp in his arms. He puts it into the back of his pickup and disappears into the house again.

"See, a robber!" Trevor whispers in a disgusted tone.

"Shhh, don't say anything. We'll just walk by, and I'll try to get the license plate number." Mr.

## Shelter from the Storm

Ward's face looks grim. "You always have people who take advantage of the misery of others," he mumbles.

Just then the man appears again, this time carrying a box. "Ah-choo!" It sounds loud. He stops, looks at the three across the street, and starts grinning. "Hi, kids, back again?" he says with a smirk on his face. "I saw you, just a minute ago, peeking through the broken windows."

Mr. Ward walks across the street, the twins following right behind him.

"You're probably wondering what I'm doing here, right?"

Trevor does not know what to say, and Alisha tries to hide behind the neighbor.

"I thought you were a . . ."

"I was what?"

"A robber!" Trevor whispers.

The man bursts out laughing. "Just as I thought!" He slaps him on the shoulder. He points to the shattered flowerpots in the box and the broken lamp on the pickup. "Do robbers usually take these types of things?" he asks.

Trevor smiles shyly, shaking his head.

"I am glad you are watching my mother's house, son. I'll tell my mom she does not have to

## Chapter Eight

worry about robbers, with the two of you around. Ah-choo!"

The twins don't know what to say. This time Alisha pulls Trevor along. "Let's go," she says softly.

When they come home, Grandma and Grandpa are ready to leave. The whole family is standing near the little white car.

"There they are! Where have you been?" Mom asks. "You know you may not leave without permission! When Grandma and Grandpa are gone, you go inside, right away!"

The twins quickly kiss their grandparents good-bye.

"Look, Grandpa, all the dents and scratches on your car," Trevor says when Grandpa is sitting behind the steering wheel.

Grandpa smiles out of the window: "A car is just a car, my boy. It still drives. We were all spared. That's more important, right? Every time when I see the car, it will remind me of this special time I had in Grandbrook."

With a last "Goodbye" the little white, dented car disappears round the corner.

# CHAPTER NINE

It is Sunday. Church has not started yet. The organ is playing softly. Trevor sits in the corner next to his Mom, Alisha on the other side. She can see her grandma coming in to sit in front of them. She always walks in by herself. Grandpa is not in church yet. He comes in with the minister, the elders, and the deacons because he is a deacon.

When the service begins, the minister reads from the Bible: Isaiah 32. Alisha listens. It talks about a storm too.

After the long prayer they sing Psalter seventy-six:

## Chapter Nine

The voice of Jehovah, the God of all glory
Rolls over the waters; the thunders awake
The voice of Jehovah, majestic and mighty
Is heard, and the cedars of Lebanon break.

"The collection today is to cover the costs of the storm damage," the minister says. Alisha looks back at Mr. and Mrs. Van Baalen. They sit two pews behind them. Their house was split in two by the twister.

Her mom nudges her. Oh, yes, she may not look behind her in church. Grandpa comes with the bag. When Alisha gets it, she has to hold on to it tightly. She has never seen it this full.

The minister begins to speak: "The text for today is Isaiah 32:2a. 'And a man shall be as a hiding place from the wind.' We may still be here today," he says. "That is a great wonder. The Lord has spoken strongly during this week. It looked as though His patience had come to an end, and He would have been just. All our sins speak against us. When we saw the dark clouds twirling Tuesday at ten after three, there was not much time to escape. But in God's judgment there was such great mercy. He spared our lives. The

## Shelter from the Storm

tornado is past, but as long as you don't have a new heart, you are still in danger.

Children, God is still warning you. Where did you try to hide Tuesday? In the basement? Under the tractor? In the ditch? Was that your shelter from the storm? Today I may point you to a better hiding place, to the only hiding place: The Lord Jesus Christ. Beg the Lord to open your eyes so that you may see who you are. Ask Him also to show you Him, who is the Refuge for sinners, the Hiding place from the wind. Flee to Him with all

## Chapter Nine

your sins. Only in Him can you find rest and safety."

It is very quiet in the church as the minister preaches. The time goes by fast. When the minister says "Amen," Alisha is surprised. Is he finished already? Often she finds it hard to listen in church, but today it wasn't.

When they come home, they get orange juice and a piece of apple pie.

"Do you still remember what the minister preached about?" Father asks.

"O yes!" they all answer.

"About the storm, and about the hiding place," Trevor says.

"Do you still remember Who is the hiding place, Alisha?"

"The Lord Jesus," Alisha answers.

"When I was in school, I learned a little poem," Mom says. "It also talks about the Lord Jesus and the storm. It goes like this:

"Thus, when the storm of life is high,
Come, Savior, to my aid;
Come, when no other help is nigh,
And say, 'Be not afraid.'"

## CHAPTER TEN

It is two days later. Mom is reading the Grandbrook Gazette. Alisha is cutting pictures out of wrapping paper. She will glue them on stiff paper to make cards. Trevor is playing on the floor with his trucks. He pretends they are cleaning up after the tornado. One is the dump truck, another one the wood chipper.

"Look in the paper, Alisha. It's all about the tornado," Mom says.

Together they look. Mom reads aloud:

"Tornado hit Grandbrook."

"It happened very quickly, almost without warning. Stormy, wet, and windy weather gave

## Chapter Ten

way to thirty seconds of terror in Grandbrook when a funnel cloud touched down in the west end of the village at 12 minutes after 3 p.m., Tuesday, June 29.

And then there was sunshine. By 3:30 p.m. Grandbrook residents had already begun to clean up the debris the tornado had left behind. In all, forty-three houses and barns were damaged by the twister. There were no serious injuries during the storm."

### Shelter from the Storm

Mom turns the page. Alisha looks at the pictures.

"Look, Mom. This is our school. That is Mrs. Finnans' house, and here. . . ."

Suddenly Mom starts smiling. "Read this, Alisha!" she says, and she points to a little ad. Alisha leans over the table and reads slowly:

"A blue autograph book was found in the front yard of Patrick and Patsy Field's home at 19 Willow Lane, following the recent tornado. The book is owned by a girl named Alisha. It has a picture of a white bear on the cover and two clasps holding the pages together. If you know to whom the book belongs, call the Grandbrook Gazette at 521-2373."

Alisha looks at her mother with shining eyes. "Oh, Mom!" she says: "They found my book!"

She gives Mom a big hug. "Can you please call right away?" she begs.

Mom takes the newspaper, walks to the phone, and dials the number. She does not have to wait long. Alisha is all ears while Mom is speaking. Too bad she can't hear the other person talking!

"We may pick it up this afternoon around four o'clock," Mom says when she gets off the phone.

## Chapter Ten

"We had better take the car because it's out in the country. You know that farm where they always have all those white ducks in the yard? I think that's where it is."

The time goes too slowly for Alisha. She constantly glances at the clock.

Mom notices how restless Alisha is. "Please, do something. Otherwise, I'll put you to work! Why don't you help me fold my wash?" Alisha smiles. She loves sorting laundry. She puts the towels on one pile, the socks on another. The pile with the kid's clothes is always the highest.

Finally it is a quarter to four. When they leave the house, it is pouring rain.

"Run to the van, and don't jump in the puddles," Mom says. Raindrops splash and bounce on the sidewalk. They pound on the roof of the van. Water trickles off the trees. The grass is soaking wet.

They jump into the van. Alisha and Trevor sit in the back.

Alisha looks through the window up at the sky. It looks dark. "Do you think we're getting a tornado again?"

Her mother, who is busy getting Brian in his car seat, turns around. "I don't think so.

## Shelter from the Storm

Tornadoes usually come when it is very humid. It's not warm at all."

The twins look outside during the drive. Much of the debris is cleaned up already. In some places people are still busy.

"Rainbow! Rainbow!" In his car seat, Brian points outside. Sure enough! Looking out from her side of the car, Alisha sees a brightly colored rainbow.

"That's because the sun is shining, and it's raining at the same time," Heidi explains. "Daddy says: If you want to see the rainbow, you should stand with your back to the sun."

Alisha watches the beautiful colors: orange,

## Chapter Ten

red, yellow, green, blue, purple. "Where do all those colors come from, Mom?"

"Do you remember where we read about the rainbow in the Bible?"

"When Noah came out of the ark," Trevor says. "My teacher told about it in school, too."

"That's right. God promised that the earth would never be destroyed by a flood anymore. There often is a rainbow after a storm. It appears when the sun has come out to shine again, but there is still a little rain in the air. Whenever we see the rainbow, we may always think about that promise of the Lord," Mom says.

When they arrive at the duck farm, it has stopped raining. "Wait in the car for a minute," Mom says. "I'll check first whether this is the right place."

A little later she comes back with a friendly young man. He has a brown cap on and is chewing on a toothpick. He points to the gravel road that runs through the field.

Mom steps into the car again. "Thank you very much," she smiles and closes the door.

"It's not here, but there must be a little farm behind those trees over there." They drive onto the bumpy gravel road.

## Shelter from the Storm

"See those tree stumps in the field?" Heidi points. "A whole row of about eight tall trees is down. Unbelievable!"

The road is getting bumpier all the time. Sometimes Mom really has to slow down to avoid holes in the road. Now they cross a railway track.

"I don't think many trains come through here anymore," says Trevor when he sees the grass growing between the tracks. The gravel turns into sand. They pass a garbage dump where some raccoons are climbing into the rubble.

"If I were not sure it was here, I would have turned back," Mommy says. Finally, when they drive around the corner, they see a really old farmhouse with some rickety sheds.

A man with white hair under a grey hat and a pipe hanging from the corner of his mouth, is holding a shovel in his hand. He puts it down and walks to the car. "Come on in," he bellows, "My wife has the tea ready. We love visitors."

Mom gets Brian out of the car seat and together they walk to the house.

Inside, they find a sweet old lady, sitting on a kitchen chair, a cat on her lap. "There you are! Make yourself at home." She points to the couch.

## Chapter Ten

"Don't mind these books here on the floor. My husband is sorting them out. He loves books. He always goes to garage sales to find more. There's never an end to it. I used to go along also. Then my husband would pile up books in the front seat, and I would sit in the back." She tickles the cat behind his ears. "Cindy, you had better get off

my lap. I have to serve tea first." The cat jumps down and lies in front of the door.

"And who is Alisha? What a beautiful autograph book you have! I looked through it and read it all. I still remember some of the poems from when I was young. I liked the picture of that puppy too. What a cutie!"

The lady looks around, a puzzled look on her wrinkled face. "Where did I put the album? I'm sure it was lying here this morning. I hope my husband didn't clean it up with some of his old

## Chapter Ten

books. Oh, here it is, on top of the fridge." She hands the book to Alisha.

Alisha's eyes sparkle. She looks at her book. It's a bit dirty, but that doesn't matter at all.

"Thank you very much!" she says to Mrs. Field.

"I found it in my garden. Why did it blow away?" Patsy Field asks in a friendly tone.

"I left it outside, on the picnic table," Alisha whispers shyly. " Then the tornado came."

Brian puts up his hands. "Tomato! Tomato!" he cries out happily. The lady laughs. "You are a smart little guy."

When they come home, Alisha flips through the book. Then she skips to her mom who is frying meat for supper in the kitchen. Alisha holds up her book. "I'll never leave it outside anymore, Mom," she says, heaving a big sigh, "Never!"

## CHAPTER ELEVEN

It's two weeks later. A little white dented car comes driving around the corner. "Grandpa, Grandma!" Everyone runs outside, including Brian on his little bare feet.

As soon as Grandpa is sitting in his chair, Alisha comes with her book. "Now you had better write in it quickly!"

"Alisha!" Dad scolds. "Can't you have a bit of patience? They are just here. And that's not the right way to ask either."

Alisha bows her head. "Will you please write in my book?" she asks softly.

Grandpa smiles. "What about a cup of coffee first? And then you find me a pen."

## Chapter Eleven

Alisha beams. Sorting through the drawer, she finds one. With her autograph book in her lap, she sits besides Grandpa's chair. Grandpa strokes her hair. "Waiting takes so long, doesn't it? Especially for my little girl."

Soon he seats himself at the kitchen table. She watches him as he takes a paper out of his pocket. Grandpa unfolds it. "I thought you would ask me to write in your book tonight. So I made up a little poem at home." Alisha looks over his shoulder as he writes in nice curly letters:

## Shelter from the storm

Our life is full of sin.
We can't do any good,
An evil heart within,
Not living as we should.

God's storm of wrath comes soon.
That time is close at hand.
If God should mark our sin,
O Lord, we couldn't stand.

Is there a place to go?
A shelter where to flee?
Christ is the only hiding place.
The Rock of rest is He.

Alisha sighs when Grandpa is done. "That's nice, Grandpa. It's about the tornado."

"About the storm and about the shelter, the shelter from the storm," he says.

Alisha nods.

"Now you have to go to Grandma," Grandpa says. "She told me that if I would write in your album, you would like to have some pictures in it as well."

## Chapter Eleven

Alisha skips to Grandma. She is in the living room, knitting a sweater for Brian.

"Grandma, Grandpa wrote really nicely in my album. He told me you have some pictures for it."

"Give me my purse. They should be in there." She opens her wallet and takes out some stickers—colorful flowers growing in the field. "You don't need glue for these. Just take the back paper off, and you can stick them in your album. Here, let me do it for you." Grandma puts them in nicely and gives the book to Alisha. "Happy?" she asks. Alisha nods. Her eyes are beaming.

When it is time to go to bed, Alisha takes her album along. This time it does not take long for her to fall asleep. When her mom comes upstairs a little later, she calls the others. "Come, have a look at Alisha."

They all tiptoe into her room. There she is, sleeping on her back, a smile on her face. Her hand rests on her pillow. And in her hand? A blue autograph book with a white bear on its cover.

Mom takes it away carefully, and lays it on Alisha's night table. For a moment there is a little frown on Alisha's face. She opens her eyes.

## Shelter from the Storm

"Good night, Alisha," Mom whispers, "Good night!"

Alisha smiles again. She turns onto her stomach and before Mom leaves the room, she is sound asleep.

# OTHER BOOKS AVAILABLE

*The Flight from the Enemy.* By Alien Mol.

"The Germans are coming!"
Quickly David motions Rachel and Hannah to hide in the haystack. He has to help Father and Mother! They are in the house. Will they be able to hide in time? Finally the Germans leave. The children hurry back to the house. It is completely silent. They call for Father and Mother, but there is No answer. They are all alone. The girls sobbed. What must David do now? Where must they go now?

ISBN 0-9670728-0-8     71 pages     softcover     7–10 yrs.

*The Mystery of the Necklace.* By Alie Vogelaar.

Going to a new school often means that you do not immediately have new friends. That was also the case with Paul. And yet there is a classmate who is concerned about the "new boy." John isn't swayed by his classmates and befriends Paul. Sometimes, however, it seems that there is something between him and Paul, and yet it is not only because of the fact that Paul never goes to church.
In the school the classmates even whisper that Paul is a thief . . .

69 pages     hardcover     8–12 yrs.

*Margreet Series:* by Alie Vogelaar.

| | |
|---|---|
| *Not so High, Margreet!* | ISBN 0-9670728-2-4 |
| *What are your Plans, Margreet?* | ISBN 0-9670728-3-2 |
| *At Last . . . Margreet!* | ISBN 0-9670728-4-0 |

These books are 120 pages or more and hardcover.
Girls—14–18 yrs.
(Two more Margreet books hope to be printed in the future.)

## Eddie and Lydia Series: by Alie Vogelaar

A Shot Through the Window      ISBN 0-9670728-1-6
No Place to Go      ISBN 0-9670728-7-5

These books are 110 pages and hardcover.
Boys and Girls 10–16 yrs.
(Two more Eddie and Lydia books hope to be printed in the future.)

## The Hasty Promise by Alien Mol

Cherie Mason is fifteen years old and a sophomore in high school. Because of her attitude she at times makes it difficult for herself. But not only because of that, nasty comments are thrown at her. She adores the handicapped Mike in the hospital as well as the adorable daughters of the not so liked teacher Mr. Fayson. For this reason she is called the teacher's pet. When the boys in the class want to take revenge, Cherie is hasty in making a promise. This promise gives her plenty of trouble, especially when her conscience begins to speak. However, she has to keep her promise.

ISBN 0-9670728-8-3      110 pages    hardcover    Girls 12–16 yrs

## A Great Miracle in a Small Mountain Village by Marian Schalk

This story happened a long time ago, in a small village. That village lies in the middle of the mountains in Germany. The people who lived there are poor. Walter no longer has a father; That is why his mother has to work on a farm. One day something very bad happens. Grief comes into Walter's house. They have to suffer from hunger. Doesn't the Lord take care of them? Yes, a great miracle happens there. The God of Elijah is still alive!

To be read to children from four years old and up. To read by themselves for boys and girls from six years old and up.

ISBN 0-9670728-9-1      48 pages    softcover    4–8 yrs.

**EARLY FOUNDATIONS PUBLISHERS**